KU-337-490

Schools Library and Information Services

S00000645934

Cinderella

First published in 2001 by
Franklin Watts
96 Leonard Street
London
EC2A 4XD

Franklin Watts Australia
56 O'Riordan Street
Alexandria
NSW 2015

DUDLEY PUBLIC LIBRARIES

L 46156

645934 SCH

JY WAD

Text © Barrie Wade 2001
Illustration © Julie Monks 2001

The rights of Barrie Wade to be identified as the author
and Julie Monks as the illustrator of this Work have been
asserted in accordance with the Copyright, Designs and
Patents Act, 1988.

A CIP catalogue record for this book is available
from the British Library.

ISBN 0 7496 4045 6 (hbk)
ISBN 0 7496 4228 9 (pbk)

Series Editor: Louise John
Series Advisor: Dr Barrie Wade
Series Designer: Jason Anscomb

Printed in Hong Kong

Cinderella

by Barrie Wade

Illustrated by Julie Monks

W
FRANKLIN WATTS
LONDON•SYDNEY

Once upon a time there was a beautiful young girl called Cinderella.

Cinderella had two ugly stepsisters who were very cruel to her.

They made Cinderella do
all the hard work.

The two ugly sisters were
invited to the Prince's ball
at the royal palace.

Cinderella wished that she
could go too.

Suddenly, a fairy appeared.
"I'm your fairy godmother,"
she told Cinderella.

She waved her magic
wand ...

Cinderella's rags turned
into a beautiful dress.

On her feet were sparkling
glass slippers.

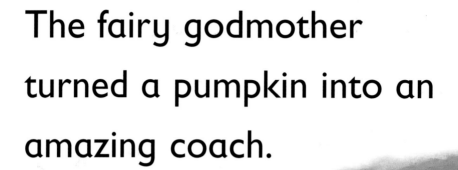

The fairy godmother
turned a pumpkin into an
amazing coach.

Then she turned some
mice into horses.

"Have fun," she said to Cinderella, "but be back by midnight or else!"

"Thank you!" cried
Cinderella.

At the ball, everyone
wondered who the
beautiful princess was.

The Prince danced every
dance with her.

When the clock began to strike twelve, Cinderella suddenly remembered.

She ran back to the coach
but lost one of her glass
slippers on the way.

Then the coach and
horses disappeared.

Cinderella's beautiful dress
turned back to rags.

The next day the Prince set
out to find Cinderella again.

Every girl in the kingdom
tried on the glass slipper ...

... but it didn't fit.

The ugly sisters tried to fit into the slipper but their feet were much too big.

"Let this girl try," said the Prince when he saw Cinderella.

"But that's only Cinderella," cried the ugly sisters, "the slipper won't fit her!"

But it did!

So the Prince found his
Princess and they lived
happily ever after.

Leapfrog has been specially designed to fit the requirements of the National Literacy Strategy. It offers real books for beginning readers by top authors and illustrators. There are 21 Leapfrog stories to choose from:

The Bossy Cockerel
Written by Margaret Nash,
illustrated by Elisabeth Moseng

Bill's Baggy Trousers
Written by Susan Gates,
illustrated by Anni Axworthy

Mr Spotty's Potty
Written by Hilary Robinson,
illustrated by Peter Utton

Little Joe's Big Race
Written by Andy Blackford,
illustrated by Tim Archbold

The Little Star
Written by Deborah Nash,
illustrated by Richard Morgan

The Cheeky Monkey
Written by Anne Cassidy,
illustrated by Lisa Smith

Selfish Sophie
Written by Damian Kelleher,
illustrated by Georgie Birkett

Recycled!
Written by Jillian Powell,
illustrated by Amanda Wood

Felix on the Move
Written by Maeve Friel,
illustrated by Beccy Blake

Pippa and Poppa
Written by Anne Cassidy,
illustrated by Philip Norman

Jack's Party
Written by Ann Bryant,
illustrated by Claire Henley

The Best Snowman
Written by Margaret Nash,
illustrated by Jörg Saupe

Eight Enormous Elephants
Written by Penny Dolan,
illustrated by Leo Broadley

Mary and the Fairy
Written by Penny Dolan,
illustrated by Deborah Allwright

The Crying Princess
Written by Anne Cassidy,
illustrated by Colin Paine

Cinderella
Written by Barrie Wade,
illustrated by Steve Cox

The Three Little Pigs
Written by Maggie Moore,
illustrated by Rob Hefferan

The Three Billy Goats Gruff
Written by Barrie Wade,
illustrated by Nicola Evans

Goldilocks and the Three Bears
Written by Barrie Wade,
illustrated by Kristina Stephenson

Jack and the Beanstalk
Written by Maggie Moore,
illustrated by Steve Cox

Little Red Riding Hood
Written by Maggie Moore,
illustrated by Paula Knight